What's SPECIAL About ME, Mama?

words by
Kristina Evans

pictures by
Javaka Steptoe

 JUMP AT THE SUN BOOKS • NEW YORK

Printed in Singapore • Reinforced binding • First Edition • 10 9 8 7 6 5 4 3 2 1 • F850-6835-5-10349
Library of Congress Cataloging-in-Publication Data on file. • ISBN 978-0-7868-5274-1 • Visit www.disneyhyperionbooks.com

To
HALEY FAITH COLLIER
Loving you always;
inspired by you constantly;
blessed by your presence continuously . . .
Hugs and kisses, Mommy

—K.E.

What's special about me, Mama?

So many things, Love.

Like what, Mama?

Like your eyes, Love,
and the way they tell
AMAZING
stories without any words.

Your skin, Love, and the way the colors blend together

to create the most BEAUTIFUL autumn earth.

But Daddy and I have the same color skin. . . .
What's special about *me*?

Your hair, Love, and the way it springs right back into place after a swim in the tub.

But Grammy's hair does the same thing. . . .
What's special about *me?*

Your freckles, Love,
and the way the sun kissed your nose and cheeks
with just the **PERFECT** amount.

But Auntie Jade has freckles, too. . . .

What's special about *me*?

The way you say "please" and "thank you" when someone offers you something.

But sometimes I forget, and you have to remind me. . . .
Please, Mama, tell me what's special about me!

Your laugh, Love,
and the way your laughter
fills the house with
JOY.

It's just like when sun
fills the sky on a cloudy day.

But some days the sun
forgets to come out. . . .

What else, Mama?

Your hands, Love,

and the way you help me in the kitchen.

But I'm too little to use the stove.
I can only mix. . . .

What else?

Your kind heart, Love,
and the way you share your toys at the park.

But sometimes
I feel like keeping
all my toys to myself. . . .

What else, Mama?

Your hugs, Love.

No one snuggles better in my arms than you do.

But . . .

And your kisses, Love,

the way they stay on my cheeks all day—

they make me feel so BIG and STRONG.

But those are little things, Mama. . . .

Those are far from little things, Love.

Hugs and kisses are two of God's greatest gifts.

What's special about you, Love,

is that you are

LOVED

more than

ANYBODY

in the

WHOLE WIDE WORLD—

by me!

Tell me **AGAIN**, Mama.